From the movie

Disney FROZEN

Holiday Annual 2015

EGMONT
We bring stories to life

First published in Great Britain in 2015 by Egmont UK Limited,
1 Nicholas Road, London, W11 4AN

Written by Catherine Such. Designed by Jeanette Ryall

© 2015 Disney Enterprises, Inc.

ISBN 978 1 4052 7839 3
59990/1
Printed in Italy

This Frozen Holiday Annual belongs to:

....

Write your name here.

From the movie

Disney FROZEN

All this inside ...

Meet the Characters

Let's find out more about your Frozen friends and their magical, wintery world.

Marshmallow

Marshmallow is a large snowman that guards the ice palace. He is a very strong and menacing henchman ready to do everything for Elsa.

Sven

Sven is Kristoff's loyal friend and helper. Young Kristoff saved Sven's life and the two have been inseparable ever since. Sven pulls Kristoff's sledge.

Kristoff

Kristoff is a loner mountain man. He makes his living as an ice harvester and is accompanied only by his reindeer, Sven.

Princess Elsa

Princess Elsa is the first-born child in the royal family of Arendelle. She's a natural leader and the Kingdom loves her, but she has the power to create ice and snow. It's a dangerous power because it's controlled by Elsa's emotions, so she tries to protect Anna by avoiding her.

Princess Anna

Princess Anna is the second-born child in the royal family of Arendelle. She's loving, optimistic and fearless, but she feels alone and strives to connect with her big sister, Elsa, who has shut her out.

Olaf

Olaf is a funny little snowman created by Elsa. Olaf has a very big heart and strives to be useful. He loves warm hugs and his biggest wish is to see summer.

Snowflake Count

Elsa has made it snow. How many of each colour snowflake can you count?

Can you trace the trail this snowflake has made with your finger or a pencil?

Write your answers in the boxes.

Answers on page 67.

10

Colour Elsa

Use your prettiest pens to
colour this magical picture.

Seaside Search

Olaf is dreaming of summer. Can you spot the items below in the picture?

Add some bright colours to the kite.

Who would you send a postcard to?

To Anna & Elsa,

Having a lovely time on the beach. It's very hot. Wish you were here.

Love Olaf xx

Anna's Act of Love

1 I'm Princess Anna of Arendelle. My older sister, Elsa, is the Queen. She ignored me for most of my life until I told her Prince Hans and I were engaged. That got her attention! She was so upset she blasted ice across the room and eventually froze the kingdom! When she ran away, I had to follow.

2 I found Elsa in a beautiful ice palace. I asked her to come home and thaw the kingdom but she screamed that she didn't know how. Her icy powers seemed to burst from her body ... and hit me by accident!

3 Elsa created a giant snowman to chase me and my friends Kristoff and Olaf away from her frozen palace. We escaped, but I had a problem - I was getting colder and colder!

4 Kristoff took me to the trolls for help. They were very wise so I hoped they'd know what was wrong with me. But I was shocked when a very old troll said I would soon freeze completely! Only an act of true love could save me.

5 I hurried home to find my prince. His kiss would be the act of true love I needed. But Hans wouldn't kiss me! He had only been pretending to love me to become the ruler of Arendelle. Now that I was almost frozen, Elsa was the only one standing in his way.

6 Hans locked me in the library. I was so cold I could barely move. I thought I'd never see my sister again and I couldn't warn her about Hans! I was feeling hopeless ...

7 ... Until Olaf showed up and helped me escape! He said Kristoff loved me and that it was his kiss that would save me. I headed into the storm to find Kristoff, but instead I found Hans, about to strike Elsa with his sword! I couldn't let him hurt her!

8 Instead of going to Kristoff, I ran to stand in front of my sister. And that's when I turned to ice!

But a moment later, something incredible happened – I began to thaw! My act of love had saved me! It also made Elsa realise that love was the key to controlling her powers – now she knew how to bring summer back to Arendelle. The Kingdom was saved!

The End

Who's Next?

Look at the pictures below. Can you work
out which character comes next
in each sequence?

a.

b.

c.

Answers on page 67.

Ice Magic

Elsa has created some magical giant snowflakes. Trace the dots to finish the biggest snowflake.

Add some pretty colours to the other snowflakes or, for extra magic, add some glitter.

Tricky Teasers

See how quickly you can help
Olaf solve these fun
snowman puzzles.

Which is Wrong?

Which Olaf picture is the odd one out?

a

b

c

Busy Bees

Follow the trail the bees have
made with your finger.

22

Playtime Pals

Who does Olaf want to play with? Copy the letters into the matching coloured boxes to find out.

N V
V E
S E

☐ ☐ ☐ ☐

Sunny Days

Olaf is dreaming of summer. Circle the items below that he might need on a sunny day.

Oops, Olaf!

Olaf has fallen apart! Help put him back together by counting his body parts.

Picture Match

How well do you know Frozen? Can you match the film pictures to the correct descriptions?

Which film picture doesn't have a description?

1

2

3

4

5

Answers on page 67.

Answers on page 67.

a

Olaf dreams of summer and all the fun things he can do.

b

While trying to save Elsa, Anna is frozen solid.

c

Elsa unfreezes Arendelle and restores summer time to the town.

d

Elsa becomes Queen and ruler of Arendelle.

Palace Puzzles

Join the princesses in their palace to solve these royal teasers.

Special Guest

Cross out the letters that appear twice to reveal who is visiting the sisters at the palace.

E S R T
O V T N
OR A A

_ _ _ _ _ _ _

Beautiful Blooms

The bees love Anna's flowers. How many can you count?

Answers on page 67.

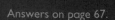

Size Sort

Can you put these tiaras in order of size, starting with the smallest?

a

b

c

d

e

Snowstorm

Which characters are hidden behind these snowflakes?

a

b

c

d

Sisters Forever

Are you more like Anna or Elsa?

Colour the snowflake next to your favourite picture in each question, then add up your totals to find out.

Anna   **Elsa**

1 Which season do you prefer spring or winter?

2 Which hair colour do you like more red or white?

3 Which of these patterns do you like?

4 Which is more powerful - friendship or magic?

Total

It's Amazing!

Help the sisters get back together by guiding Anna through the snowflake maze to Elsa.

Start

Finish

Answers on page 67.

29

Frozen Fun

Use your own magical powers to complete these icy puzzles!

Chilling Out!

Match the jigsaw pieces to the spaces to finish this snowy scene.

Find the Friends

Can you find the names of these friends hidden in the wordsearch?

A	N	O	L	A	F	E
K	R	I	G	O	L	F
C	O	A	K	E	N	D
D	H	N	V	L	V	B
C	T	N	M	S	U	S
M	O	A	V	A	O	V
S	V	E	N	C	G	E

Colour a snowflake as you find each one.

 ANNA

 ELSA

 SVEN

 OLAF

Skating Sisters

Use the small picture to help you colour
Elsa and Anna on the ice.

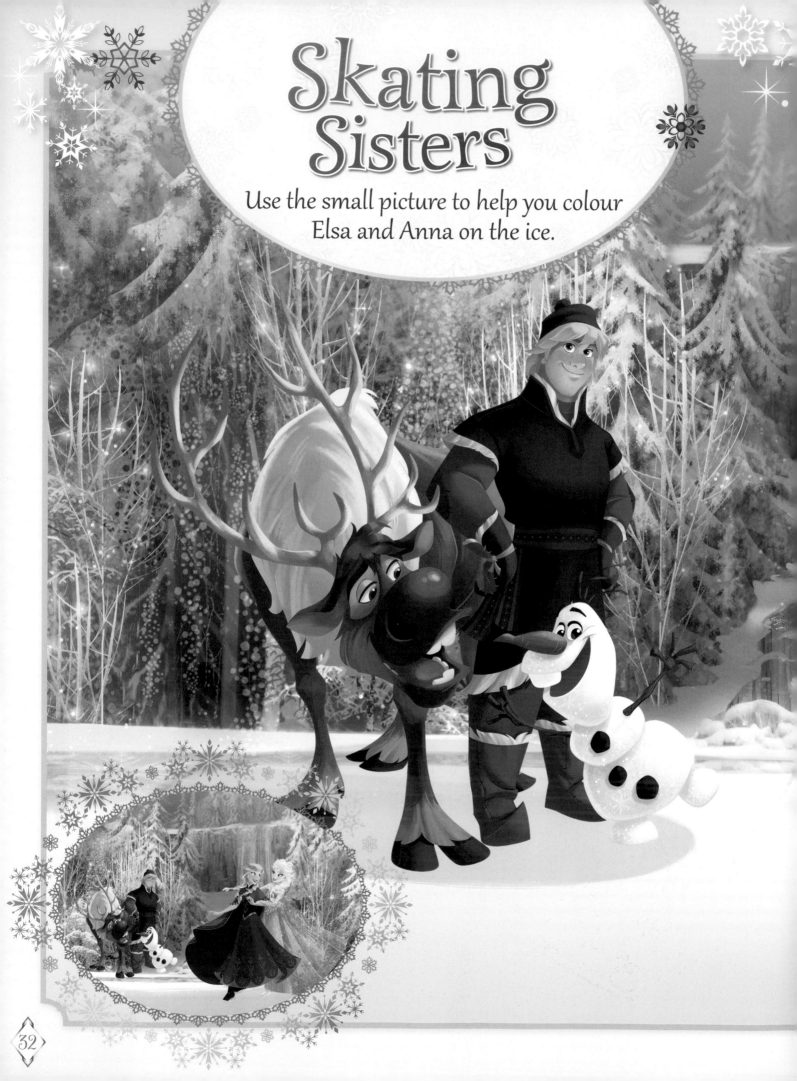

Sparkling Snowflakes

Anna and Kristoff are in a snowstorm.
Answer the questions below
to help them.

b

a

h

1
Which snowflake
is the smallest?

2
Which two
snowflakes match?

3
Which snowflake
is the biggest?

4
Which snowflake
is the same colour
as Anna's hair?

Which is your favourite snowflake?

Answers on page 67.

Help Olaf

Olaf has lost an arm! Which path does he need to follow to find it?

Answers on page 67.

Olaf Says ...

Olaf says lots of lovely things but which of
the quotes below wasn't said by him?

"I'm Olaf and
I like warm hugs!"

"I've always loved
the idea of summer!"

Colour the
flower next
to the correct
quote.

"Do you want to
build a snowman?"

"Some people are
worth melting for."

Snowy Differences

Anna, Kristoff and Sven are trekking to the Ice Palace.

Trace the names of the things that each character is thinking about.

sledge   Elsa   carrot

Can you find six differences in picture b? Colour a snowflake as you spot each change.

a

b

Answers on page 68.

Frosty Fun

See how quickly you can solve
these Frozen word puzzles.

Mysterious Message

Anna has left a message for Elsa.

Cross out all
words that are
COLOURS in the
grid below to reveal
what it says.

GREEN	DO	ORANGE	YOU
WANT	RED	TO	YELLOW
BUILD	PURPLE	BLUE	BROWN
PINK	A	SNOWMAN	WHITE

Anna's message is:

....

....

....

Fill in the Blanks

Can you fill in the missing letters to finish writing the names of your Frozen Friends?

_nna

_lsa

_ristoff

_ven

Word Wheel

Can you find four wintry words in this word wheel?

Start

S N O W I C E F R O S T C O L D

Answers on page 68.

Perfect Gift

Olaf has made a present for Anna.
Use the colour code to work out
where he has hidden it.

What do you
think Olaf's present
is? Give it some
magical colours.

Answers on page 68.

Colour Anna

Anna looks lovely in her beautiful dress.

Colour this picture with your favourite pens.

Elsa's Icy Magic

1 I'm Elsa, Queen of Arendelle. My coronation was a disaster, thanks to my sister, Anna. We were arguing about her engagement to Prince Hans and I accidentally froze everything in sight! Everyone thought I was dangerous, so I fled to the mountains and built a magnificent ice palace.

2 I was happy to be free to use my power. Then Anna arrived. At first I was pleased to see her but then she told me I'd frozen the entire kingdom. I didn't know how to unfreeze it! Suddenly, I lost control of my magic and accidentally hit her with an icy blast.

3 Hans and the guards arrived next. I tried to use my magic to defend myself. Hans said people would believe I was a monster if I used my icy power, so I stopped. Then the guards captured me!

4 Back in Arendelle, I was locked in the dungeon. Hans warned me that some people wanted to punish me for freezing the kingdom. He said I needed to bring back summer but I didn't know how.

5 To make matters worse, Anna had not returned home. I knew I was a danger to her and to Arendelle but I was trapped. I felt so frustrated.

6 Then suddenly I lost control of myself! Icy blasts burst open my chains and crumbled a dungeon wall so I could escape into the storm. All I could think about was taking my magic far, far away.

7 But Hans appeared and told me that my sister had perished. When I had accidentally hit her with my icy blast, I had frozen her heart! Devastated, I fell to the ground and the storm stopped. Hans raised his sword ...

8 ... and suddenly, Anna appeared and jumped between Hans and me! The sword hit her instead - and broke! Anna was frozen solid!

 I wrapped my arms around my frozen sister and wept for all the years we'd spent apart. Then something amazing happened – Anna thawed and hugged me back! I had found my sister again and I was never going to let her go.

The End

What's Wrong?

Use some magic to help you spot the odd one out in each of the rows.

1

a   b   c   d

2

a   b   c   d

3

a   b   c   d

Answers on page 68.

Picture Puzzle

Use the picture clues to help Olaf complete this crossword.

One answer has been added to help you.

2 B U C K E T

Down

1
2 ✓

Across

2   3   4

Answers on page 68.

Arendelle

Anna and Elsa are having a busy day at Arendelle harbour. Can you spot the close-ups below in the picture?

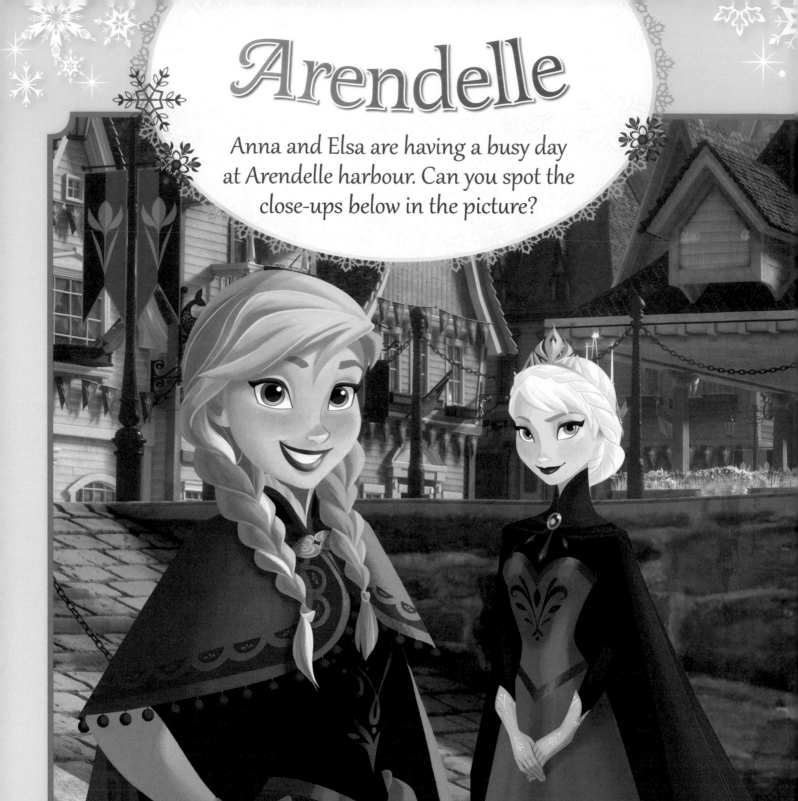

Colour a snowflake as you spot each one.

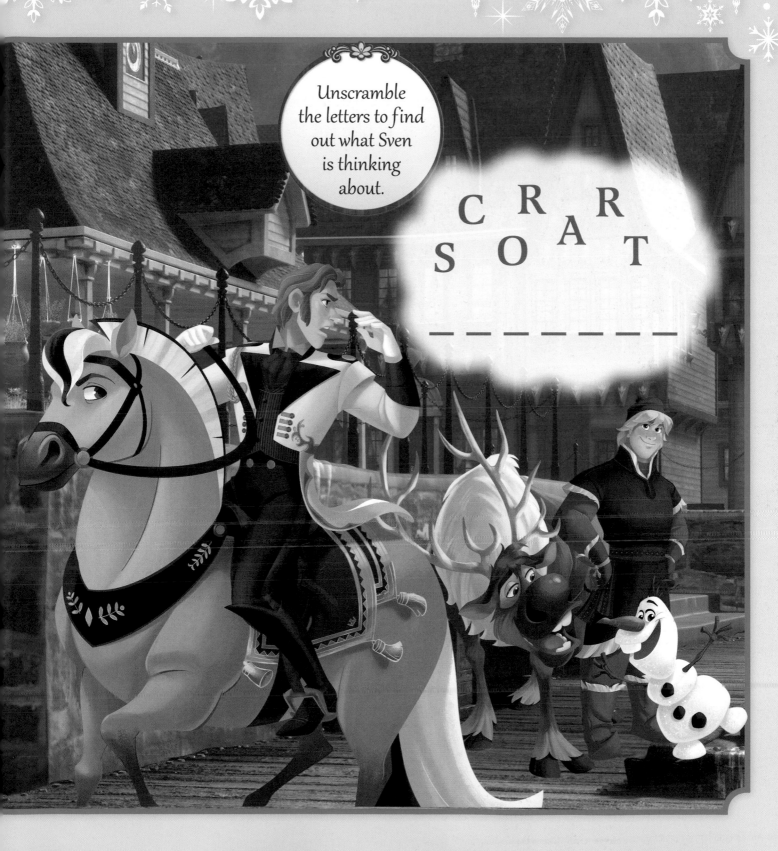

Unscramble the letters to find out what Sven is thinking about.

C R R
S O A T

_ _ _ _ _ _

Answers on page 68.

On the Move

Anna and Kristoff are looking for Elsa. Use the key on the right to guide them to the Ice Palace.

Start

Finish

Key

= Up

= Right

= Down

Answers on page 68.

Winter Wonderland

Can you find the characters below
hidden in this icy scene?

Answers on page 68.

56

Mirror Magic

Kristoff has written a message for Anna. Hold this page up to a mirror to reveal what it says.

Let's go on a sledge ride!

Try writing your own mirror message in the space below.

Answers on page 68.

57

Shadow Match

Draw lines to match the characters to their shadows.

1

2

3

4

a

b

Which shadow doesn't match a character?

e

c

d

Answers on page 68.

Build Olaf

Sometimes Olaf has trouble keeping himself together! Use these pieces to make him whole again.

You will need:
Scissors · Glue
· Piece of paper
· Your imagination!

1. Carefully cut out the pieces along the blue dotted lines.

2. Arrange your Olaf pieces in whatever way you like.

3. Glue your Olaf pieces onto paper to complete your own unique snowman.

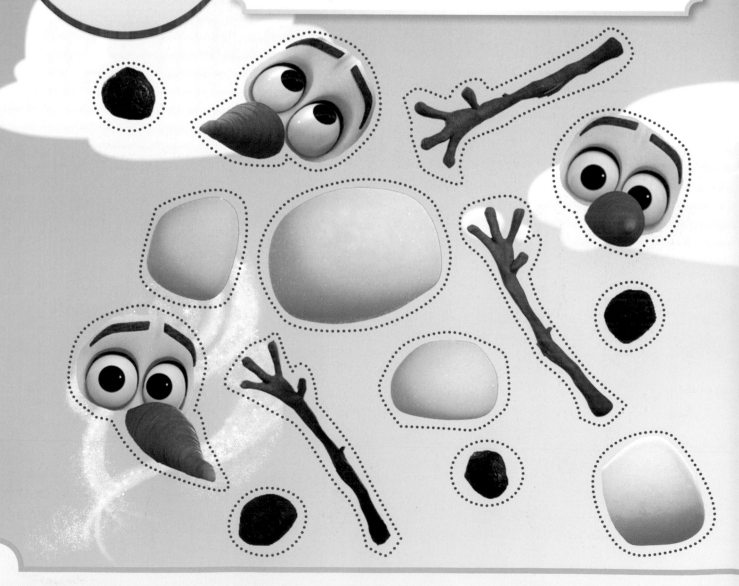

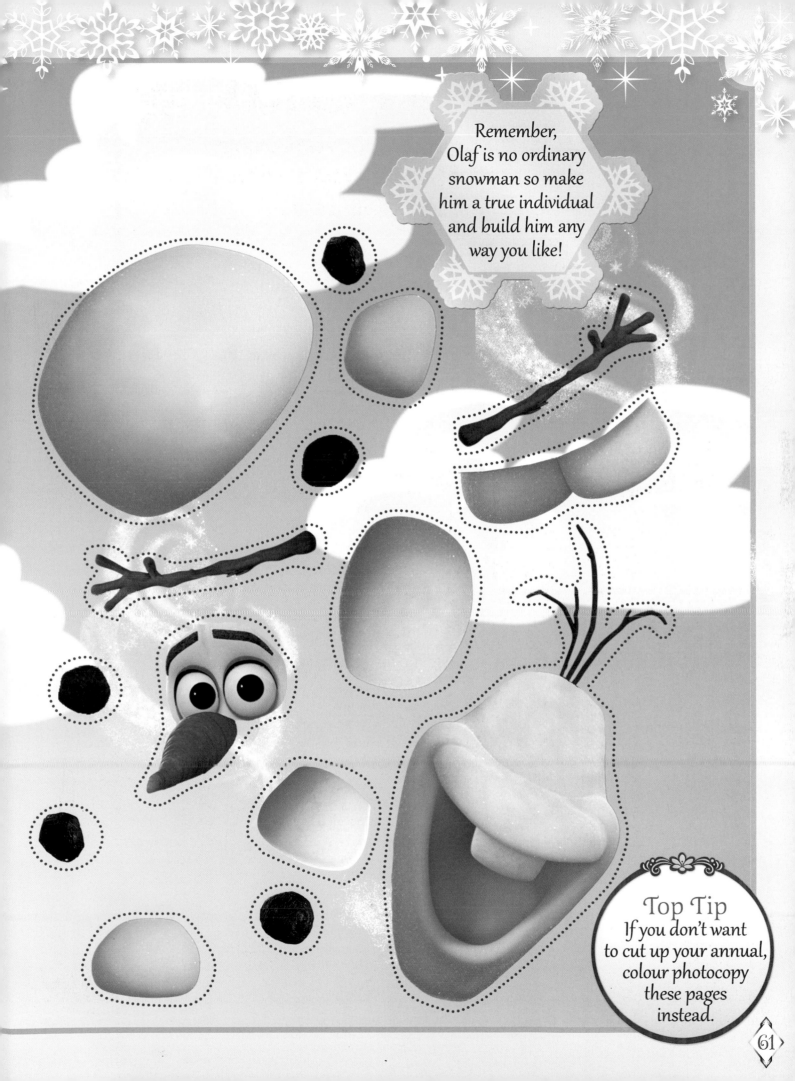

Remember, Olaf is no ordinary snowman so make him a true individual and build him any way you like!

Top Tip
If you don't want to cut up your annual, colour photocopy these pages instead.

61

Which Way?

Kristoff wants to visit the trolls but he's lost his way. Guide him through the maze to his friends.

Start

Finish

Sisterly Love

Colour this picture of Anna giving
Elsa a great big hug.

Cool Quiz

Answer these questions then add up
your score to see how big a
Frozen fan you are.

1
Who is the Queen of
Arendelle?

a   b

2
Who pulls Kristoff's
sledge?

a   b

3
Who pretends to be in
love with Anna?

a   b

4
Which sister is the
youngest?

a   b

5
Who creates the
Ice Palace?

a   b

The results
Turn to page 68 for the correct answers. Then
add up your score and check your result below.

0-1 correct - Uh-oh, you'd better watch
your Frozen DVD again!

2-3 correct - Not bad, you're on your
way to becoming a Frozen expert!

4-5 correct - Amazing, you know
Frozen as well as Anna and Elsa!

From the movie
Disney
FROZEN

Cut along here.

Answers

Page 10
Snowflake Count

Write your answers in the boxes.

| 6 | 4 | 3 | 5 |

Page 20
Who's Next?
a – Anna, b – Kristoff, c – Elsa.

Page 22
Tricky Teasers
Which is Wrong?: **b.**
Playtime Pals: **Sven.**
Sunny Days: **Sunglasses, sunhat, parasol.**
Oops, Olaf!: **7.**

Page 24
Picture Match
1 – d, 3 – b, 4 – c, 5 – a.
Picture 2 doesn't have a description.

Page 26
Palace Puzzles
Special Guest: **Sven.**
Beautiful Blooms: **There are 10 bees.**
Size Sort: **b, d, c, e, a.**
Snow Storm: **a – Olaf, b – Kristoff, c – Anna, d – Sven.**

Page 28
Sisters Forever
It's Amazing!

Start

Finish

Page 30
Frozen Fun
Chilling Out!: **1 – b, 2 – a, 3 – c, 4 – d.**
Find the Friends:

A	N	O	L	A	F	F
K	R	I	G	O	L	F
C	O	A	K	E	N	D
D	H	N	V	L	V	B
C	T	N	M	S	U	S
M	O	A	V	A	O	V
S	V	E	N	C	G	E

Page 34
Sparkling Snowflakes
1 – d, 2 – h and l, 3 – m, 4 – f.

Page 36
Help Olaf
Path b.
"Do you want to build a snowman?" wasn't said by Olaf.

Answers

Page 38
Snowy Differences

Page 40
Frosty Fun
Mysterious Message: **Do you want to build a snowman?**
Fill in the Blanks: **1. Anna. 2. Elsa. 3. Sven. 4. Olaf.**
Word Wheel: **snow, ice, frost, cold.**

Page 42
Perfect Gift
Olaf has hidden Anna's present in the castle.

Page 50
What's Wrong?
1 – c, 2 – b, 3 – d.

Page 51
Picture Puzzle

Page 52
Arendelle
Sven is thinking about carrots.

Page 54
On the Move

Page 56
Winter Wonderland

Page 57
Mirror Message
Let's go on a sledge ride!

Page 58
Shadow Match
1 – a, 2 – c, 3 – b, 4 – d.
Shadow c is the odd one out.

Page 62
Which Way?

Page 64
Cool Quiz
1 – b, 2 – b, 3 – b, 4 – a, 5 – a.